1998

Thursday 4 — PLUMBER

B. BACK LATE

1:00 CLINIC

MUM!

MAGGIE WILL

JENNY PICKUP 9:00

Friday 5 — PICK UP /

CANCEL MAIL — ASK MICKY & JAKE TO FEED AN... 6:00 BE...

BILL 12:...

Saturday 6 — (FILM)

Sunday 7

REPORT DUE 31/6

BLUE MIST VINYL
MOONSHADOW EGG SHELL
DROP CLOTHS

DAY OFF   ASSEMBLY 12:00
MON 1 PICK UP DRY CLEANING   JAKE CIRCUS 3:45-4:15
        BUGS FOOTBALL 4:30

BEGIN WORK AT 5:30 ——— 8:30

Jake & JOSH TO BIDDIE 5:00 SUPPER

DRY CLEANING !!!

ER WHA H. ♡

TO MAGGIE TO SLEEP
PICK UP J: FROM MUSIC LESSON
5:30 / 8:30 4:00 TEA AT BIDDIES

...WERS FOR B & B
...B   BIKE SERVICE
W 5:30-11:30 MELE BEA TO .IT

WITH BILL
PAINT KITCHEN
JOSH PICK UP BIKE 11:15

GET KEY FROM
Biddie of al-LEAVING 10:30 ish

REMIND J TO FEED RABBIT & G. P.S

BLUE MIST
ROLLER REPLACEMENT
SMALL BRUSH

DOG FOOD
CAT FOOD
PLANT FOOD
FURNITURE POLISH
MUSIC WORKBOOK

JAM
BIKE BELL
COCOA
CHIPS
COKE

HOW TO RESTORE WOOD
PUBLISHED BY BAILEY HEAD

JUGGLING BALLS

...Y CLEANI...
...ELINA

Bill
Biddie
Bea
Bugs
Boo Boo + Bear
Granny Bea

For Frances
J.O.

1 3 5 7 9 10 8 6 4 2

Copyright © Jan Ormerod 1998

Jan Ormerod has asserted her right under the Copyright, Designs and Patents Act, 1988,
to be identified as the author and illustrator of this work

First published in the United Kingdom 1998 by
The Bodley Head Children's Books, Random House,
20 Vauxhall Bridge Road, London SW1V 2SA

Random House Australia (Pty) Limited
20 Alfred Street, Milsons Point, Sydney,
New South Wales 2061, Australia

Random House New Zealand Limited
18 Poland Road, Glenfield,
Auckland10, New Zealand

Random House South Africa (Pty) Limited
Endulini, 5A Jubilee Road, Parktown 2193, South Africa

Random House UK Limited Reg. No. 954009
A CIP catalogue record for this book is available
from the British Library

ISBN 0-370-32356-4
Printed in Singapore

Jan Ormerod

Who's Who In Our Street?

JENNY
JOSH
JAKE
JOCK

Maggie
Me!
Micky + Molly

The Bodley Head
London

Breakfast here,

lunch there,

and over here for tea.

Jump down, Cat!
You belong to us all in our street.

It's Monday morning. Schooltime.

Josh is a racer.

Moll and Bugs are lazy bones.

Mel and Bea chatter and natter, but they do keep an
eye on Micky and Jake.
There's always someone to walk with in our street.

Micky's sick and Maggie is at work,
so Biddie and Boo Boo take him home.

At school, Mel, Bea and Josh sing,
and at work, Maggie gives Granny Bea a ring.

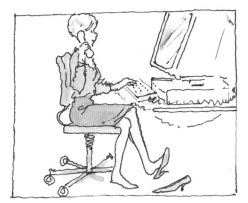

'Come to lunch
on Sunday?'

After school, Jenny takes Jake to circus class.

Then she posts the letters, pays the bills,
collects the cleaning
and buys a book for Micky.
Don't forget the apples for Biddie.
Don't forget Bugs.

Football is finished!
Someone is always lending a hand on our street.

Mel and Bea take Molly to the dentist,
then do homework.

Josh is watching the telly.
Someone is being lazy on our street - and we all know who that is!

It's Tuesday, after school. Bugs plays with Molly.
Maggie kisses her better when she
scrapes her knee.

Micky plays with Jock while
Jake practises the piano.
Josh is trying to watch the telly.

Bugs, Molly and Boo Boo look after the pets
while Maggie and Bill go shopping.

The big girls are doing homework (and this time it's true).
Biddie will help them if they need her.

Nearly time to eat.
The cheese needs grating.
The table needs laying.
The shopping needs unpacking.
Who's being helpful on our street?

And whose turn is it to wash up?

On Wednesday night, when Jenny goes out
she wears Biddie's skirt and Maggie's shoes.
Who paints her nails?
Who puts on her make up?

And who gets the most excited?

On Thursday Granny Bea visits with a hat for Boo Boo.
Molly sits on her lap. Jake shows her his juggling.
Bugs has painted a picture, and Mel and Bea have made a cake.

Who do we love to see in our street?

On Fridays, when Jenny works late,

Jake sometimes sleeps here,
or sometimes sleeps here.

Tonight, Josh is in charge,
and Mel and Bea are helping out.

Who is looking after whom?
And who ate Jock's supper?

When Mel, Micky and Molly go to their dad's for the weekend,
Maggie may go for a walk in the sun

or the rain.

'Hi Mel, it's me!'

Who gets the muddiest?

Some weekends Bill keeps an eye on everyone
while the mums do the garden.
(They like doing that in our street.)

This Saturday, Bill takes Bugs, Boo Boo, Molly, Micky,
Jake and Jock to the park to play while Biddie has a rest.
Mel and Bea do homework, and Josh watches the telly.

Maggie helps Jenny. 'That looks better.'
Who is most tired at the end of the day?

Bad dog, Jock! That naughty cat!
Maggie shouts and Jenny cries.
Bugs and Molly get the giggles.
Jake and Micky get cross.
Boo Boo screams.
And Mel and Bea come running.

Josh makes everyone a mug of tea and cleans up.

Who's a good boy, then?

It's Sunday. Bill, Biddie, Bea, Bugs and Boo Boo are off on holiday.

Who has lunch with Granny Bea?
Who waters the plants?

Who cuddles the rabbit? Who cleans out the guinea pigs?

Who misses their friends?

DEAR ALL—
WE MISS YOU! I
WISH YOU WERE
HERE. THE BEACH
IS GREAT!
LOTS OF LOVE—
BIDDIE   X
BILL   X X
BEA   X
BUGS   X X
BOO BOO   X
(and BEAR) X

MAGGIE, MEL, MICKY,
MOLLY, JENNY, JOSH,
JAKE, JOCK & CAT
c/o MRS. BLUE
19 THE AVENUE
BROOKLANDS

And who is pleased to be back
together at the end of the week?

All of us
in our street!

Monday
15

9:30 PLAYGROUP *BOOTS! BUGS

MUM TO SIT STAY OVER
DINNER JENNY +14 — 7:0

Monday
15

dinner Jenny's 7:30 —
       meet H/
Mel + Bea baby sitting   # chocs

day
10:30 Coffee Jenny
2:00 bank Manager
3:45 Molly + Bugs to part

day

6:00-8:00 computer class

to father's 6:30

Biddie + Bill to

mum—
I'm sorry I
was grumpy!
Love,
Mel

TOSFAX